MY RED, WHITE, AND BLUE

Written by **ALANA TYSON**

Illustrated by **LONDON LADD**

PHILOMEL

FOR AIDAN, ELI, AND IZZY, MY INSPIRATIONS. MAY
YOU ALWAYS FIND STRENGTH IN YOUR VOICES. —A. T.

TO ALL THE FATHERLY AND BROTHERLY FIGURES IN MY
LIFE. I WOULDN'T BE THE MAN I AM WITHOUT EACH
ONE OF YOU. THANK YOU. —L. L.

PHILOMEL BOOKS
An imprint of Penguin Random House LLC, New York

First published in the United States of America by Philomel Books,
an imprint of Penguin Random House LLC, 2023

Text copyright © 2023 by Angela Alana Halidou
Illustrations copyright © 2023 by London Ladd

Philomel Books is a registered trademark of Penguin Random House LLC.

Visit us online at penguinrandomhouse.com.

Library of Congress Cataloging-in-Publication Data is available

Manufactured in China

ISBN 9780593525708

10 9 8 7 6 5 4 3 2 1

RRD

Edited by Talia Benamy
Design by Ellice M. Lee
Text set in LTC Cloister

Artwork created using acrylics, textured cut paper, tissue paper, and colored pencil.

This is my flag; it represents me.

A symbol of freedom and hope's what I see.

I'm American-born; my family is, too.

So we show off our pride waving red, white, and blue.

Our flag greets our neighbors, and strangers, and friends.

It jumps in the breeze as it waves and extends.

A hearty salute every morning is due,

as I ride in to learn some things old and some new.

From the bus I wave hi to the people I know,
Mr. Ming in his shop, Dr. Smith on the go.
My flag is theirs, too, and I'm happy to share.
Our community's strong, full of people who care.

At circle, we're different as different can be.
Miss King says our flag promotes *DIVERSITY*.
Your teacher is right, said my grandpa to me,
but there's also much more to *that flag's history*.

He said long, long ago, when his dad was wee small,
Old Glory did not represent us at all,
with her beautiful stripes and those twinkling white stars.
America's history left long-lasting scars.

While our flag can mean promise, and refuge, and glory,
for some folks, it tells a complete different story.
While she waves in the wind and invites all to stay,
there were many who didn't see things quite that way.

WHITES ONLY

The North and the South were divided in view.
One side wanted freedom for all, not a few.

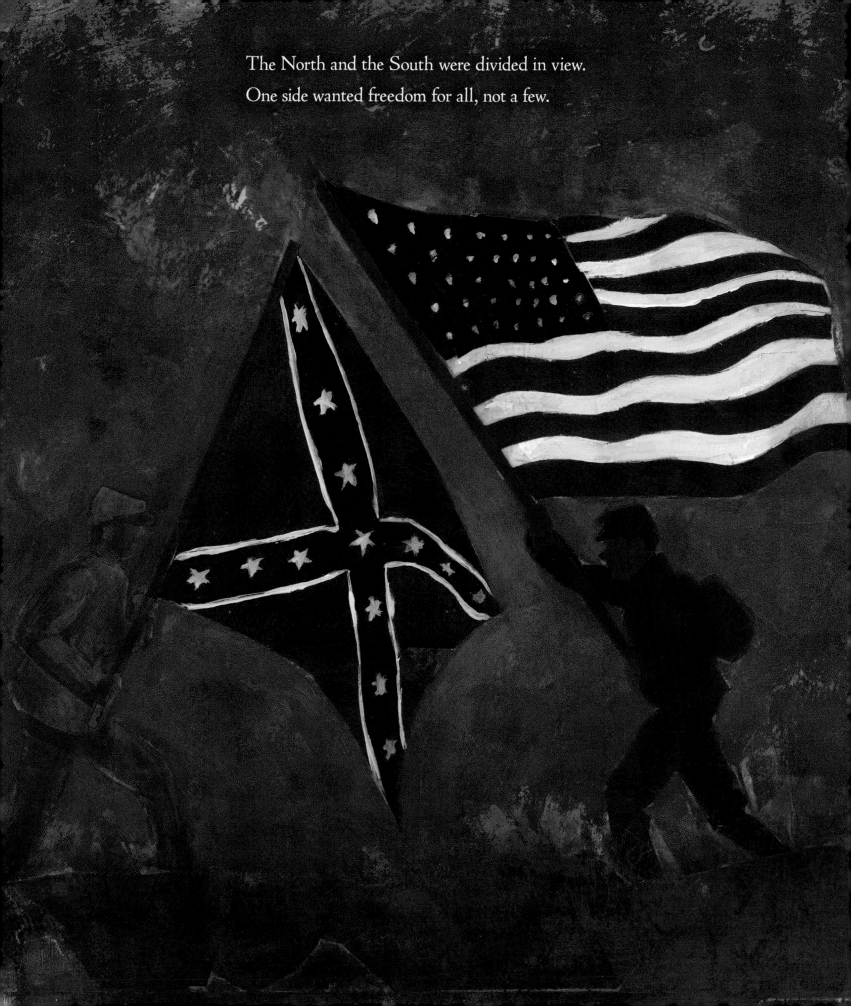

And when the North won, millions yelled, *We are free!*
But then came a new call . . . for equality.

Many stood in the streets, brave and calm for the fight,
asking only for change and demanding their rights.
After sit-ins, and marches, and protests, and songs,
today we STILL fight, and there's much that's STILL wrong.

So when the flag flies, some decide not to praise.
Instead they refuse in a number of ways.
A fist in the air, kneeling down on one knee,
a silent head bow while they sit quietly.

There's no justice for all, so we choose not to stand.
We will not sing the anthem, we won't raise our hands.
A protest that's silent, yet public and grand.
A message that many may not understand.

Grandpa said, *Child, it is their right not to sing,*
but there's lots 'bout that flag and the pride it can bring.
Obama and Tubman, Goines, Martin, and Parks:
they helped shape this country and all left their marks.

My ancestors helped make America great.
That's a matter of fact, and there is no debate.
An entire museum in DC tells our story,
how we're weaved in each stitch of that faded Old Glory.

Still, showing your pride might sometimes seem tough.

On days like that, know: what you feel is enough.

To praise our flag, Grandpa said, is a choice.

It's for you to decide, it's how you use YOUR voice.

So at school, and at games, and whenever I can,
I CHOOSE to salute, with my heart and my hand.
I'm my ancestors' dream, what they hoped to be true
A brown child who'd find pride in the red, white, and blue.

AUTHOR'S NOTE:

PATRIOTISM IN THE BLACK COMMUNITY

For as long as there has been a United States of America, there has been inequality for Black people within it. Even after the Civil Rights Movement, which resulted in more rights for Black people in this country, things weren't really equal. Starting in 2013, a movement called Black Lives Matter brought greater attention to this ongoing issue, especially to the deaths of many Black people at the hands of law enforcement. The leaders of this movement demanded to know why the United States wasn't doing more to prevent racism. More and more, Black communities were losing faith in the country's ability to honor the line in our Constitution that states, "All men are created equal." Many Black people didn't feel equal at all; they struggled to find their patriotic voice amid layers of injustice.

In 2016, a football player named Colin Kaepernick refused to salute the American flag during the national anthem. Instead, he stood up for Black communities and the need for racial justice by kneeling in a silent protest. Kaepernick was not demonstrating hate for the flag. He was simply hoping society would take notice and listen, and understand that people who looked like him needed to be heard.

Other athletes have used their fame to highlight social inequality, too. In 1968, Tommie Smith and John Carlos, two Black track-and-field Olympic athletes, made a statement just like Kaepernick's. During the national anthem while receiving their medals, they bowed their heads and raised gloved fists in the air, calling attention to the need for racial equality in the United States. The iconic photo is one of the most recognized images in American sports history. In an interview years later, Smith stated that their action wasn't about the flag itself at all; instead, they had simply used a moment and a public stage to point out a problem. "It was a cry for freedom and for human rights. We had to be seen because we couldn't be heard," said Smith.

For all three of these men, their acts were courageous but costly. Kaepernick was fired from the NFL. Smith and Carlos were banned from the Olympics and suspended from the US team, and their medals and endorsements were taken away. Fifty-one years later, in November 2019, Smith and Carlos were inducted into the US Olympic and Paralympic Hall of Fame, a decision made by the US Olympic Committee that also served as a public apology.

But while some Black people may choose a silent protest, others are more comfortable with publicly embracing their American heritage and displaying patriotism. There are so many Black civil rights leaders, politicians, inventors, historians, educators, veterans, and artists who give Black Americans plenty of reasons to express pride not just in Black history, but in American history as a whole, and that is definitely worth celebrating.

Whether it's saluting the flag, engaging in a silent protest, or finding some other way to use your voice, know that your unique voice has power, and it's up to you to use it in the way that feels best to you.